THE SEVEN AND FATHER CHRISTMAS

Enjoy another thrilling adventure with the Secret Seven. They are Peter, Janet, Pam, Colin, George, Jack, Barbara and, of course, Scamper the Spaniel.

There were two fifty-pence pieces in the money Colin's mother gave him for her Christmas shopping – but the strange thing was, they didn't weigh the same. This discovery sets the Secret Seven on the trail of a sinister forgery racket. Surely all the Father Christmasses in town can't be involved? The Seven waste no time in trying to trace the source, but will tracks in the snow lead them to the unknown forgers in time, or will the forgers find them first?

D0774175

The Seven and Father Christmas

A new adventure of the
characters created by
Enid Blyton, told by Evelyne
Lallemand, translated by
Anthea Bell

Illustrated by Maureen Bradley

KNIGHT BOOKS
Hodder and Stoughton

First published in Great Britain by Knight Books 1986
Third impression 1987

British Library C.I.P.

Lellemand, Evelyne
    The Seven and Father Christmas: a new adventure of the characters created by Enid Blyton
    I. Title   II. Bradley, Maureen   III. Les Sept ne croient pas au Père Nöel. *English*
843′.914[J]   PZ7

ISBN 0 340 39975 9

Printed and bound in Great Britain for Hodder and Stoughton Paperbacks, a division of Hodder and Stoughton Ltd., Mill Road, Dunton Green, Sevenoaks, Kent TN13 2YA.
(Editorial Office: 47 Bedford Square, London WC1B 3DP) by
Cox & Wyman Ltd., Reading

CONTENTS

Chapter One

COLIN'S INTERESTING DISCOVERY

Colin's mother was on the telephone, talking away to Peter and Janet's mother about the Christmas party that was being held in the village hall. It was for the old folk who lived in Honeysuckle Cottages.

'Yes, please do bring two dozen mince pies, and I'll make another batch myself,' she was saying. As she talked into the receiver, she was playing with one of the brightly-coloured decorations hanging on the Christmas tree in one corner of the sitting-room. 'And I'm making a couple of Yule logs — that was Colin's bright idea!' She smiled at Colin, who was sitting at the big desk. 'He thought the old people would like a nice chocolate Yule log. Now, we must get in touch with Jack's mother too — I know she said she'd make some sandwiches, and so will Pam and Barbara, I'm sure, but we must decide who uses what fillings, and . . . '

Colin sighed. When his mother started talking on the telephone, she seemed to go on and on for hours. It was his bad luck the phone had rung just then, so he had to wait, and couldn't go out until the conversation was over. Like the rest of the Secret Seven Society, he thought it was a very good idea for the mothers and fathers to have a Christmas party for the old people whose cottages the Secret Seven had saved, when they were threatened with demolition in the summer. However, he did wish Peter and Janet's mother could have rung up *after* he went out shopping and not before. His own mother had been dictating a whole long list of things she needed, and she had given him the money which was now in a little pile on the desk. But before she could finish the list the telephone rang, and she asked him to wait before she picked up the receiver.

'Won't be a minute!' she whispered now, as Peter and Janet's mother talked away at the other end of the line.

Colin sighed. *He* knew what his mother's 'minutes' were like! He began spinning the coins on the desk as if they were tops, seeing how long he could keep them going.

Now his mother was discussing the little presents they were planning to give the old folk! Sighing again, Colin started playing with his father's letter scales, which stood on the desk. To kill time, he weighed first a pencil, then an eraser, then a roll of adhesive tape, and then, one by one, the coins he was about to take shopping.

The twenty-pence coin and the five-pence coin both weighed about five grams, and a ten-pence piece weighed twelve grams. He weighed a few more twenty-pence, ten-pence and five-pence pieces, then a pound

coin, and then he came to two big fifty-pence coins. He weighed one fifty-pence coin, waited for the needle on the letter scales to stop quivering, then he took it off the scales and weighed the other . . . and then he suddenly stopped and stared.

'My word!' said Colin to himself. 'It's not as heavy as the other fifty pence!'

Just to make sure, he put the first coin back on the scales and checked that it really did weigh considerably more than the second – at least four grams more – although it looked just the same every other way. They were both shiny new coins with the same date on them.

Colin didn't let his surprise show. Glancing at his mother, he realized that from where she stood she couldn't see his little experiment. She and Peter's mother seemed to have finished their discussion of the old people's party for the moment, but still she hadn't rung off. And while she was telling her friend about the nice photograph of Colin's little brother with Father Christmas that she'd had taken outside Bailey's department store in the nearby market town, Colin himself was deciding he must keep those two fifty-pence pieces for himself.

He had a feeling there was something peculiar and interesting about them!

That afternoon the Secret Seven met in their usual place, the shed in Peter and Janet's garden. Scamper the golden spaniel was there too, of course. As soon as his mother had at last completed the shopping list, Colin had gone straight round to see Peter and tell him about his interesting discovery. Then he went to do his mother's shopping while Peter, as the leader of the Seven, made sure everyone else knew a meeting was being called.

It wasn't very warm in the shed in winter time, but the Seven were all well wrapped up as they sat there. Almost all, that is, because they were still waiting for one last person to arrive – the one who was nearly always late!

'Trust Pam!' groaned Jack. 'Honestly, she's *never* on time for anything!' He was getting impatient, like the rest. They couldn't wait to find out why a meeting was being called today.

A moment later, there was a knock at the door. 'Password?' called Peter, signing to the others to be quiet.

'Fifty plus fifty make twenty-eight!' announced Pam, through the door. 'Really, what a *silly* password!' she added, coming in, and smiling at the others. 'I don't know who thought up that one. It doesn't make any sense!'

Peter looked rather crossly at her as he closed the door behind her. 'I'd have thought it made sense to *you* all right,' he said. 'You seem to think fifty minutes means an hour, as often as not!'

Everyone laughed at Peter's joke, and after that nobody could really feel cross with Pam, specially as she joined in the laughter herself. She sat down with the others.

'Now,' said George eagerly, 'what's all this about, Colin?'

Colin jumped up and began talking excitedly. 'Well, you see, the reason why fifty and fifty make twenty-eight is that a fifty-pence coin weighs fourteen grams, so two fifty-pence coins weigh twenty-eight grams, only this morning I found a fifty-pence piece which only weighed ten grams, so in other words fifty and fifty made twenty, four each less, if you see what I mean!'

'No, I don't!' confessed Janet. 'Colin, I don't understand a word of it!'

'Nor do I,' agreed Barbara. 'And I bet Scamper doesn't, either.'

'Why don't you begin again, and give yourself a moment or so to take a breath now and then?' suggested Jack.

'More haste, less – ' said George.

'Speed!' Colin interrupted. 'I know, I know! Well, *I* think you're all being a bit slow on the uptake!' He sounded rather annoyed at the thought of having to repeat something which was perfectly clear to *him*.

'Look, let me do it, Colin!' said Peter. 'You explained it all when you came round this morning to tell me.'

'If you like,' said Colin, not very pleased, as he sat down with the others again.

Peter stood up, patted Scamper to tell the spaniel to stay put, and then waited until the others were ready and listening. When there was complete silence, he started talking, taking his time and not sounding as over-excited as Colin.

'Right, pay attention!' he told the others. 'While Colin was waiting for his mother to finish talking to my mother on the telephone this morning, he passed the time by weighing some coins on his father's letter scales. Got that?'

Everyone nodded.

'Good,' said Peter. He went on: 'He had weighed several coins when he came to two fifty-pence pieces among the money his mother had given him for her

12

shopping, and this is the funny part – they didn't weigh the same.'

'Goodness me!' said Pam, sounding intrigued.

'That's right,' put in Colin. He wasn't going to let Peter have *all* the fun of announcing *his* discovery, not if he could help it!

'And that's why I asked you all to bring as many fifty-pence coins as you could find with you,' Peter went on.

'So that we can weigh them,' added Colin. And he showed them his father's letter scales, which he had brought with him.

'Here are two,' said Janet, taking them out of her pocket. 'That's all I had in my money-box.'

'I've got five!' announced Barbara proudly. 'Only because I haven't done my Christmas shopping yet, though!'

The others all produced their fifty-pence pieces, talking excitedly. 'That'll do!' Peter told them. 'Don't all talk at once! Now Colin is going to demonstrate his discovery again!'

By now Colin was in a better temper. He put the letter scales on a plank over an orange box, which the children used as a table, and showed his friends the two coins. 'I had a pound in my money-box, so I used that when I was out shopping for my mother instead,' he told them.

Then he put one of the coins on the dish of the little scales. 'Look, that weighs exactly fourteen grams,' he said. He replaced it with the second coin. 'On the other hand, this one weighs just ten grams.'

13

'Yes, you're quite right,' agreed Jack. He had been watching closely as the needle on the scales quivered and finally came to rest.

'Now let's start checking by weighing Janet's coins,' suggested Colin. The little girl handed them to him.

'Fourteen grams and fourteen grams,' said Jack, bending over the scales.

'Now yours, George,' said Peter.

'Fourteen, fourteen, fourteen,' Colin read out.

Next it was Barbara's turn. Each of her five fifty-pence pieces weighed exactly fourteen grams too. So did Peter's four fifty pences, and Jack's two coins.

But when Pam put the last of *her* three coins on the letter scales, Colin uttered an exclamation of surprise.

'This one's four grams underweight as well! It's lighter than all the others – exactly like that second coin of mine!'

'I say!' said Barbara. 'There's something odd about this.'

Chapter Two

THE MYSTERY DEEPENS

'There certainly is,' George agreed. 'Pam, can I borrow that lightweight fifty pence of yours?' And he picked it up and rang it on the 'table', telling the others: 'Listen to the noise it makes!'

They all listened hard to the sound of the coin.

Then Jack did the same with one of the heavier coins. 'Hear that? They don't sound the same!'

He felt rather proud of this discovery. 'We'll have to find out what's inside them,' said Jack.

'How?' asked Pam.

'By sawing one in half!' said Colin.

'No,' said Peter, 'by sawing *two* in half. A normal one and a lightweight one. Then we can compare them.'

Wasting no time, he took a metal saw off the board where the Secret Seven kept an assortment of tools hanging on hooks. 'You never know when they might come in handy,' Peter has said when he first put up the board – and he had been quite right!

'Let's have a go at the heavier one first,' said George.

'We'd better put it in the vice – it's dangerous to saw metal if you don't,' Colin pointed out. What luck that Peter's father, seeing they had collected some tools, had given them an old vice he didn't need any more in his own workshop! Peter put one of the heavier fifty-pence coins into it, and began sawing away.

The saw made a loud, grating sound as it passed over the hard metal. Scamper, who had been sleeping off his dinner, pricked up one ear. The Seven waited in suspense.

On went the sound of the saw as the minutes passed by.

Fine, shining dust was rising in clouds from the

saw-blade.

'Looks as if you're nearly through, Peter,' said Colin.

Suddenly, half of the coin fell to the ground with a loud ringing noise.

'Here we are, then!' cried Peter triumphantly, passing it round. All the children looked hard at the straight, smooth, silvery surface where the coin had been cut through.

'Yes, Peter, but what does that tell us?' asked Pam at last. 'Except that one of us is fifty pence poorer – and I just hope that wasn't one of *my* fifty pences you went and cut in half!'

'Just wait a minute, while we do the same to the other one,' George said to her. 'Then we can see if there's any difference.'

No sooner said than done. Colin put one of the two lightweight coins in the vice – his own coin, as he pointed out to Pam, just in case she had any objections. And this time, George did the sawing.

The saw didn't make quite such a loud, grating noise as before.

'This one looks easier,' Jack noticed, watching as George sawed away. 'As if the metal was a bit softer.'

Sure enough, in a moment or so George had sawn through the coin, in only half the time it had taken Peter to saw through the first one.

'Look!' exclaimed Colin. 'There are two quite distinct layers of metal!'

'So there are,' said Barbara, who had picked up the half of the coin that fell to the ground. 'You can see a thin, shiny outside layer, but it's quite different in the middle – almost black!'

'It must be a lighter, cheaper sort of metal,' said Peter.

'Why cheaper?' asked Janet, who hadn't followed her brother's reasoning.

'Because these coins are forgeries, of course!' explained Colin. 'You don't suppose forgers would go to all the trouble of making counterfeit coins if they couldn't do it cheaper than the Royal Mint makes the real ones, do you?'

'Forgeries?' said Pam, stunned. 'But *this* fifty pence can't be a forgery!' she added rather indignantly, looking at her own lightweight coin. 'My big sister gave it to me!'

'It isn't anything to do with your big sister, Pam,' Barbara told her. 'She'll have got it from someone else, who got it from someone else, who got it from someone else – and so on. But where did it come from in the first place?'

'Yes, that's the question – and that's what we're going to try to find out!' said Peter excitedly. 'I think the first thing is for Colin and Pam to see how far back they can trace those two lightweight coins they brought to this meeting. Meanwhile the rest of us will go round and see if we can find any more – that's about all we can do for a start.'

That brought the meeting to a close. The Seven left the shed and went out into the garden. It wasn't four o'clock yet, but the light was already fading. The sky seemed low and grey.

'Looks like snow,' said George, waving to the others as he rode off on his bike.

'Yes, it does look like snow,' agreed Peter, shutting the garden gate after his friends. Then he went back to the shed. Janet was just tidying it up after the meeting.

'I rather think we're starting on a new adventure!' he told his sister. 'I wonder where *this* one will end?'

As soon as Colin got home, he went to find his mother and ask her some questions about the shopping she had done the day before. He managed to make a complete list of all the shops she had visited that day.

Pam did the same with her big sister, who was at home, and who told her that over the last twenty-four hours she'd been to the hairdresser's in the nearby town, and to a dress shop and a chemist's shop, and back in the village she had been to the Post Office, the grocer's and the bakery.

About five o'clock Pam and Colin met to compare their lists. Unfortunately there wasn't a single shop which appeared on *both* lists! That made them think that Pam's big sister and Colin's mother must have had their forged fifty-pence pieces in their purses for several days, so it was going to be impossible to find out where they might have come from.

The rest of the Seven hadn't been idle either. They had turned out their money-boxes to provide themselves with all the notes and coins they could, and then went off with their pockets full to get hold of as many fifty-pence pieces as possible. It was a good thing, they agreed, that school had only just broken up, and there had been no time to do much Christmas shopping yet, or they wouldn't have had enough money to carry out this plan!

Peter, Janet and Scamper went to the Post Office, where the girl at the counter was quite willing to give them fifty-pence coins for their change.

George just went up to people in the street and asked if they could give him two fifty-pence coins in exchange for a pound.

As for Jack, he decided to go and do the Seven's shopping for that week. If he bought a tube of pepper-mints, say, for twenty pence, and gave the shop-keeper a pound, he was very likely to get a fifty-pence piece in his change. He visited several shops, buying something small in each of them – and that was how he made an interesting discovery.

He was buying a packet of biscuits in the grocer's, and asked the woman in the shop if he could have a fifty-pence coin in his change.

'Why, yes,' she said, and then added, shaking her head, 'I really don't know what's come over people today! Everyone's going about wanting fifty-pence pieces!'

And not far off, in the bakery, the same thing happened to Barbara too. The man in front of her was buying cakes, and he asked the baker's wife if she could change several pounds into fifty-pence coins for him!

Chapter Three

A TRIP TO TOWN

'He was tall,' Barbara said excitedly, 'and he wore a hat right down over his eyes, and the collar of his coat was turned up round his chin as if he didn't want people to see his face. But I could see he had a scar on his left cheek.'

She had just been telling everybody about what she'd seen and heard in the bakery. It was about six o'clock, and the Seven had met again to compare notes. Except for Barbara and Jack, who had had the distinct impression that they weren't the only people looking for fifty-pence coins, the others had come back not exactly empty-handed — but without any more coins that were lighter than they ought to be. Every one weighed its full fourteen grams.

'It's like looking for a needle in a haystack,' said Pam gloomily.

'And even if we do find another forged coin, how are we going to find the forgers themselves?' added George. 'Money gets passed round all over the place — there's no telling where it comes from when it's been handed on from one person to another hundreds of times!'

'I'm afraid that's true,' said Peter. 'There wasn't really much point going round the village the way we did this afternoon.'

'Got a better idea, have you?' asked Colin, rather sarcastically. He was very keen on the Seven's new adventure – after all, he had been the one to start it all. He was annoyed that the others looked as if they were going to give up!

'Yes – we go and tell the police,' suggested Jack.

'That's what I *thought* you'd say! Trust you!' Colin exclaimed. 'Whenever things get the least little bit difficult you back out! Cowardly, that's what I call it!'

Colin was quite red in the face with anger.

'Oh yes?' Jack snapped back. 'And just who do you think you are – Sherlock Holmes or something? How do we know the police aren't after the forgers of these coins already?'

'Jack may be right,' agreed George. 'That man Barbara saw in the bakery could have been a plain-clothes detective.'

'Oh no – I'm sure he wasn't!' said Barbara. 'Honestly, he looked a really shady character, not a bit like a policeman.'

'There, you see? That's another reason not to give up now!' said Colin.

'Woof! Woof!' barked Scamper, apparently on Colin's side.

'Oh well, all right, let's go on investigating the mystery tomorrow,' said Peter, deciding it was time to use his authority as leader of the Seven to put an end to this argument. 'I think we may have exhausted all possible sources of fifty-pence coins here in the village, though, so if anyone is going into the town they'd better try there. We might have more luck in town.'

Little did Peter know how right he was!

It turned out that George's mother wanted him to go into the market town with her next morning. His little sister came too. His mother was doing some Christmas shopping and wanted him to help her carry parcels. George didn't mind – it was a chance to see if he could get hold of any more fifty-pence coins.

As they walked down the High Street, George's little sister stopped and pointed at the department store.

'Look – two Father Christmasses!' said the little girl excitedly. Sure enough, there *were* two of them, dressed in red with big white beards, standing at the doorway of the shop. Children were having their photographs taken with Father Christmas – one Father Christmas took the photograph while the other posed with the little boy or girl! It was obviously a new idea for attracting customers, instead of having a Father Christmas in a grotto inside the shop as usual.

'I want to see the Father Christmasses! I want to see the Father Christmasses!' cried Colin's sister, tugging at her mother's arm. One of the Father Christmasses noticed.

'What about a nice Christmas photograph of your daughter, madam?' he asked. 'Only one pound ten for a beautiful colour photographic portrait to remind you of your child this Christmas!'

He had taken the little girl's hand and was already posing with her in front of his companion.

'Well, all right,' agreed George's mother. 'But only one photograph.'

George's little sister was delighted. She kept quite still while one Father Christmas gave her a hug and the other one took the photograph. 'Watch for the birdie!' he said. 'Now, let's have a big smile!'

The camera clicked, and they told the little girl that was all. She rejoined her mother and George, while the picture was automatically developed. 'That will be one pound ten, madam,' said the photographer Father Christmas, holding out the photograph.

'Oh, what a sweet picture!' said George's mother. She was very pleased with it, and handed it to George as she took two pounds out of her purse to pay.

'And fifty, seventy, ninety pence change,' said the Father Christmas, giving her two twenty-pence coins and a fifty-pence coin.

A fifty-pence coin! George nearly dropped the photograph he was holding. This was a good start! The Seven were collecting as many fifty-pence pieces as they could, so he must make sure he kept this one! He didn't want to arrive at the garden shed for that afternoon's meeting empty-handed.

But how was he going to get that particular fifty-pence coin out of his mother's purse and into his own trouser pocket?

Luckily the problem solved itself. About ten minutes later, while George and his sister were waiting outside a newsagent's, their mother came hurrying out and asked, 'Oh, George, have you by any chance got enough ten and five-pence coins to change for this fifty? I want to buy your father a newspaper, and they're right out of change in the shop!'

George willingly searched his trouser pockets, and found enough smaller coins to exchange them for his mother's fifty pence. It was no good trying to hear if it sounded like a forged one or not in all the noise and bustle made by the Christmas shoppers – but as soon as he was home he tapped it on the brass banisters. How thrilled he was to hear that it didn't make as clear a sound as the *real* fifty-pence pieces the Seven had tried the day before! This must be another forged coin!

'Ten grams! Yes, no doubt about it, another forged one!' said Peter, weighing George's coin on the letter scales.

'Where did you get it?' asked Barbara curiously. 'We didn't get hold of any more in the village this morning – just as Peter thought, we must have cleaned the place out of them yesterday! So you're the only one who had any luck at all today.'

'I got it outside Bailey's department store,' George said, and he told his friends about the two Father Christmasses.

'Wait a minute!' said Colin suddenly. 'I say – this is interesting. My little brother had *his* photograph taken outside Bailey's with Father Christmas too – the day before I found that first forged coin!'

'Yes, that really *is* funny,' agreed Jack. 'We could be on the trail at last!'

'I'm not so sure about that!' said Pam. 'My big sister is over nineteen, and I bet you anything *she* didn't go and get her photograph taken with Father Christmas!'

'Oh dear – a false trail!' said Janet sadly – she had been quite excited by Colin's discovery, and now by George's.

'Well,' said Peter, thoughtfully, 'it just might still lead somewhere, Janet. We know the coins are in circulation. Suppose Colin hadn't noticed anything, his mother's forged coin would have ended up in a shop till somewhere, and then moved on to another customer's purse, and so on and so forth. So Pam's forged fifty pence could quite well have passed through Father Christmas's hands, even though her big sister wouldn't know anything about it.'

'You're right,' agreed Janet, admiring her clever big brother. 'All the same, it's hard to think of Father Christmas forging coins!'

Peter couldn't help smiling at that!

'Even if there are two of him, and of course everyone knows shop Father Christmasses aren't really real,' Janet hastened to add.

'But just think what a good disguise a Father Christmas costume would be for someone wanting to put forged coins into circulation!' added George. 'Nobody could be recognized under all that beard!'

'Yes, who'd suspect a kind old Father Christmas smiling at all the children?' agreed Colin.

'We would!' said Peter firmly. 'And we're going to take the bus into town and see if we can find out any more about him – or rather, them!'

Chapter Four

OUTSIDE THE SHOP

It was four o'clock that afternoon when the Seven and Scamper arrived outside Bailey's department store in the market town, which was about fifteen minutes' bus ride away from the village. The town was still as busy and full of people doing their Christmas shopping as it had been in the morning.

'There they are!' exclaimed George, pointing to the main doorway of the shop.

'We've got to be careful how we approach them,' said Peter. 'Come over here, everyone.' And he led his friends over the road to make plans in the shelter of a positive forest of Christmas trees standing on the pavement outside a greengrocer's shop.

'Yes, that's the Father Christmas who was photographed with my little brother,' said Colin, looking through the branches.

'I say – do you think they're armed?' whispered Pam.

'Oh yes, armed to the teeth!' said Jack. 'Guns hidden in their beards, I expect!'

'Don't be silly!' said Pam crossly. 'It's all very well

teasing me, but I bet you're not so sure yourself!'

She was almost shouting, she was so keen to pretend she wasn't afraid!

'Shut up, Pam and Jack!' said Peter. 'Listen, everyone, we can't stand here all afternoon. Let's separate. Jack and Colin, you go and take up a position on the pavement opposite. That news kiosk will give you a bit of cover. George and Barbara, you can take a great interest in the toys in the shop window next to the news kiosk. Take Scamper with you. And I'll go into Bailey's itself, with Pam and Janet, and watch the Father Christmasses through the glass doors.'

No sooner said than done. Looking quite ordinary and casual, the Seven began keeping watch. There really didn't seem to be anything odd going on. The two Father Christmasses were acting just like any other shop Father Christmasses. They smiled at the children who were having their photographs taken, picked them up if they were very little, patted them on the head, and they seemed to be smiling real smiles behind their big cotton-wool beards.

'Nothing doing, if you ask me,' said Colin to Jack in an undertone.

Jack sighed. 'Not much, anyway!' he agreed. 'You know, I think we may have jumped to conclusions a bit too fast. What Peter said at the meeting may just as well apply to the Father Christmasses – *they* may have been given the forged coins in their change in a shop.'

'So they may,' agreed Colin, disappointed. 'Come to think of it, we can't really be sure my mother got her forged fifty pence from them either. It could just be a coincidence that my brother had his photograph taken here the day before yesterday.'

Meanwhile, George and Barbara were standing outside the shop window, trying to look as if they were fascinated by the display of toys just inside – but it wasn't the dolls and electric trains that really interested them. However, they had their backs turned to the road, just like the other children looking into the window. It would have taken a very observant person to guess that what they were staring at so hard wasn't the toys, but the reflection of the pavement in the glass of the window. They didn't even have to turn round to see every move both Father Christmasses made.

George and Barbara stood there for nearly two hours, while the other excited children came and went – and in all that time they didn't see anything unusual. The Father Christmasses seemed to be doing their job in a perfectly ordinary way. Poor Scamper was getting rather impatient, especially when some clumsy person trod on one of his paws and made him yelp.

All of a sudden Barbara let out a cry of surprise and clutched George's arm very hard. 'Ow!' he said.

'Listen, I'm *not* dreaming!' said Barbara in a low voice.

'Nor am I!' said George, bitterly. 'Fat chance I'd have, with you pinching me like that!'

'That man – the one in the black overcoat, just crossing the road – do you see him?'

George stared into the shop window, and sure enough, he did see a man wearing a black coat and hat, just stepping off the pavement.

'It's the scarfaced man I saw in the baker's,' Barbara told him excitedly. 'He's going over to the Father Christmasses. Oh, I wonder what will happen now?'

Full of suspense, they both watched, taking no notice of the children shouting and laughing around them as they looked at the toys on display.

'Nothing!' whispered George, disappointed, as he saw the man walk straight on.

'No, wait! He's turning round and retracing his steps!' said Barbara, breathlessly. 'But I – oh!'

She couldn't help uttering an exclamation out loud

and turning round. The other children by the shop window turned too, to see what was going on, and it was amidst general laughter that the man in the overcoat fell full length on the pavement, bringing down one Father Christmas with him.

'I say – look at that!' said George, whistling. 'Those coins rolling about on the pavement – there are at least ten fifty-pence pieces among them!'

The Father Christmas was down on all fours, picking up the coins and stuffing them back in his wallet. The children hurried to help him. In all the confusion, the scarfaced man had disappeared.

'I don't think he really fell down by accident,' said George. 'He just pretended to trip.'

'That's what I thought too,' agreed Barbara.

Lying in wait behind the glass doors of the shop, Peter, Janet and Pam had been watching the whole thing. They too had seen the man in the overcoat fall down, and they noticed the large scar on his left cheek. Of course they immediately connected him with the man Barbara had seen in the baker's shop at home the day before.

'He took one coin!' breathed Pam. 'He picked it up just before he got up himself and made off!'

'So he's interested in the same thing as we are!' said Peter. 'Well, well! We're getting somewhere after all!'

'But is he a detective or a forger?' whispered Janet.

'Didn't tell us, did he?' said Peter. 'Anyway, one thing's certain, there's something fishy about these Father Christmasses. There's too much going on around them for my liking.'

'And I wonder if those fifty-pence coins were real ones or forged ones!' said Pam.

'Well, let's find out. Janet, here's two pounds – you go and get your photograph taken!' Peter told his sister.

'Why me?' asked Janet, without much enthusiasm.

'Because you're the smallest of us, of course. It'll look almost normal for you to want a photograph,' Peter pointed out. 'I mean, can you imagine *me* wanting a picture of myself being cuddled by Father Christmas?'

That made Pam laugh out loud, and even Janet couldn't help smiling a little. She could see what Peter meant! Not very happily, she took the money from her brother and went out of the shop.

George and Barbara, still standing at the shop window opposite, saw her go up to the photographer. Recognizing Janet, Scamper started tugging at his lead. He was getting very tired of waiting, and wanted a change!

And Jack and Colin, still at their post round the corner of the news kiosk, could hardly believe their eyes when they saw Janet about to have her photograph taken with Father Christmas. The flash-bulb lit up the canopy above the shop window. And a

moment later, Janet was being given her photograph and holding out the money.

The rest of the Seven – behind the big glass doors, in front of the shop window, round the corner of the news kiosk – watched in suspense as Father Christmas gave her her change.

Poor Janet! She was looking very downcast when she rejoined Peter and Pam a moment later. 'All my change is in twenties, and one ten-pence piece!' she said crossly.

'Bother!' said Peter. 'Oh well – here goes! I'll try my own luck!'

And in his turn, Peter went out of the shop and over to the Father Christmas who had fallen flat on the pavement a little while ago.

'I say, have you by any chance got two fifty-pence coins?' he asked straight out, taking a pound out of his pocket. 'I want to give my sister fifty pence to buy our mother a nice card, and I haven't any change.'

'Why, of course,' said Father Christmas, smiling. And he gave Peter just what he wanted. Peter smiled broadly, put the two coins in his pocket, thanked the man, and went back inside the shop.

Jingling the two coins together, he showed them proudly to the two girls. 'Hear that?' he said. 'Two more forged fifty pences!'

Chapter Five

ON THE TRAIL

Fifteen minutes later, the Seven were again gathered behind the forest of Christmas trees set out on the pavement. They had been careful not to attract any attention as they left the positions where they had been standing, and joined each other once more.

They were quite sure, now, that those Father Christmas costumes concealed two dangerous criminals. But that still left two big questions unanswered: how could they make quite sure their suspicions were well-founded, and how could they explain the sinister presence of the man with the scar on his face?

In fact, they couldn't quite see *what* they ought to do next, and while they were wondering a bell rang, warning customers that Bailey's was about to close, like the rest of the shops – all of which had stayed open until six o'clock that day, so that people from offices could do their Christmas shopping. Soon a crowd of shoppers flooded out on the pavements and started home. The greengrocer took the Christmas trees that hadn't been sold back inside his shop.

The Father Christmasses were taking one last

photograph of a child, and when they were sure there were no more customers waiting, they set off along the road.

'That's the end of their working day,' said Jack.

'Yes, I expect they've put plenty of forged coins into circulation today, and now they're going back to their hideout!' said George.

'I know!' said Janet. 'Let's follow them!'

'Golly, what a brilliant idea!' laughed Colin, teasing her. 'I'm sure we'd never have thought of it but for you, Janet!'

Janet made a face at him, but she hurried after the others, who had already started out to follow the two forgers.

'Come on, we must hurry!' Peter told the Seven. 'They've just turned into Mill Road!'

The children all began to run, with Scamper in front, nose to the ground. He was really glad of some exercise after all that standing about! But when they came to the corner of the road they stopped dead, baffled!

'Oh no!' cried Jack, panting for breath. 'They've gone and disappeared!'

'They must have realized we were after them,' said Barbara.

'Or they could just have had a car parked here, and they got into it and drove away,' suggested Pam. 'Unless it was a sledge with a team of reindeer, of course!'

Nobody else thought this was much of a joke. 'If you're right,' said George, 'all we can do is wait for

Bailey's to open again tomorrow morning.' He was looking very disappointed.

But just then Colin suddenly started making violent gestures, almost pushing his friends into hiding beind a parked car. 'No, look!' he cried. 'There they are – they only went into the entrance of that office building for a few moments!'

'So they did!' said George under his breath. 'To take off their costumes, by the look of it!'

'Goodness!' said Janet in surprise. 'They don't really look like criminals at all!'

Barbara was rather taken aback too. 'Why, they're not so very much older than we are!' she said.

Sure enough, a little way down the road two young men had just emerged from the entrance hall of an office building, carrying red-and-white Father Christmas costumes under their arms.

'Yes, they only went in there to take their robes off – they're wearing ordinary clothes underneath,' said Jack.

'But if they'd wanted to go unnoticed, surely they wouldn't be carrying their disguises about – they'd at least have hidden them in a carrier bag or something!' said Peter. 'I can't make it out!'

'Don't you think we'd better go on following them?' asked Colin. 'Then we may at least find out a little more!'

And the children set off, making their way cautiously from parked car to parked car, and keeping far enough behind their quarry not to be noticed.

They went down several streets, then a short way

along the bank of the river which ran through the little town, and finally they came to a square with gardens in it. The two young men stopped to talk outside a block of flats.

'I think we'd better go into the square garden,' said Peter. 'If we keep behind those hedges, we can get really close.'

A few moments later the children were hiding behind a holly hedge, quite near the two men.

'I hope they're not going to stand here talking all night!' whispered Pam. 'I'm freezing!'

She didn't have long to wait. The two young men shook hands and then turned to go in different directions.

But they had only just started when a big black car drove up and stopped beside them. Its tyres were still squealing on the frozen asphalt when two men flung themselves out of it.

'The man with the scar!' gasped Barbara.

Taken by surprise, the two young men couldn't escape, and in no time at all they had been over-powered!

Open-mouthed, the Seven were watching the whole scene through their holly hedge.

It all happened very fast, and without a word. One of the young men was violently pushed into the car, but while their attackers were trying to get the second one in, he suddenly managed to wriggle free and escape. The children saw that he was the Father Christmas who had been taking the photographs.

The young man dashed into the block of flats and

disappeared from sight. His attackers hesitated, and seemed to realize it wasn't any good chasing him once he was inside. They got back into their car, and the driver, who hadn't left the wheel, started off at once!

The whole episode had taken only about a minute, and there were no other passers-by in the quiet little square — only the Seven, who had witnessed the kidnapping.

Peter had had to hold poor Scamper's jaws closed with all his might, to keep him from barking and giving them away. The car had just left the square when the spaniel managed to wriggle free.

'Woof! Woof! Woof!' he barked, straining at his lead and leaping about. He pricked his paws on the holly leaves as he tried to get through the hedge.

'Calm down, Scamper! Stop it! You can't do anything!' Peter said firmly, holding him back, and Jack and George came to his aid as well. Scamper might have hurt himself badly if he went plunging though the prickly holly hedge. But Janet was more successful at calming the dog down, talking gently and patting him.

Only when Scamper had finally stopped barking did the Seven really absorb what they had just seen!

'Where did they take him?' wondered Jack, baffled.

'Who *is* he?' added Colin.

But of course, none of the rest of the Seven could answer that question either.

It was quite dark now, and the children turned and left the square garden. The square itself was still quite empty, with just two street lamps casting a faint light. And the evening was getting colder and colder. In a moment they reached the scene of the drama itself. Janet gasped – she had spotted a Father Christmas costume abandoned in the gutter. The long, cotton-wool beard was almost blowing away in the wind. She picked it up.

Pam's teeth were chattering. She was scared, rather than cold!

'Well, we must go and look for the other Father Christmas – the one who ran into the building!' said

Peter, pulling himself together.

He picked up the red robe with its white fake-fur trimming.

'Yes, but how?' asked George. 'We shall feel a bit silly knocking at all the doors of all these flats, asking people if they happen to have lost a Father Christmas costume.'

'And we don't even know who those two young men are,' said Jack. 'Any more than we know who the men who've just attacked them are. Are they criminals? Or are they policemen? Honestly, you know, I think this mystery is a bit too much for us. Don't the rest of you really think the best idea would be to –'

'To carry on, of course!' said Colin, angrily interrupting. 'Stop demoralizing everyone, for goodness' sake, Jack!'

'I quite agree with Colin,' said Peter. 'We can't leave the mystery unsolved *now* just when it's getting really mysterious.'

At this point Janet suddenly looked up at the sky. She had felt something soft and cold. 'Oh – a snow-flake!' she cried, as another landed on her nose.

'It's snowing!' cried Barbara.

'It's snowing! It's snowing!' shouted the rest of the Seven in chorus.

Suddenly they all felt very cheerful. Perhaps it would be a white Christmas! They turned their hands and faces up to the sky and started dancing about in the middle of the road. Scamper leaped about too, trying to catch the snowflakes, which were falling more thickly now.

The few passers-by coming home from work turned to look at the children either disapprovingly or with amusement. One of them, a man with a little pointed beard, stopped to say in a cutting sort of voice, 'It's all very well for you children, I suppose – making such a fuss about a bit of snow! Horrible stuff, I call it – cold and slippery!'

'If you ran about in it like us you'd keep warm!' Barbara told him, and the Seven went on jumping and dancing about even more wildly than before.

A moment later, however, Colin stopped short.

'Oh, look – up there on the top floor – the window

on the right!' he cried. He was pointing to a lighted window.

'Why, do you think that's him?' asked Peter, looking up. The figure of a man stood at the window. Then, all of a sudden, the light went out, and it was too dark to see any more.

'I'm sure it was him – let's go up!' said Colin. 'I recognized him – the Father Christmas who was taking the photographs. His nose was right against the window pane.'

'Then he must have been watching us,' said Pam. 'Oh dear – I wonder what he was planning to do?' she sounded scared.

'Don't be such a coward!' said Jack. 'He heard us shouting, I expect, that's all!'

'And don't forget, he must have a lot more to be scared about than you do,' George told her.

Barbara wasn't frightened – she wanted to know more about this curious business. 'Come on, aren't we going up?' she said.

'Not all at once,' Peter decided. 'Colin and Jack, you come with me. George and the girls will stay down here.'

'Same as usual!' sighed Barbara. 'We have to stay behind twiddling our thumbs while you boys go off having fun! It isn't fair.'

'*I'm* not a girl, am I?' George pointed out. 'And I don't mind staying here with you. What's unfair about it, then?'

Barbara knew when she was defeated! She gave in.

'And you can look after Scamper, Barbara,' said

Peter kindly, giving her the spaniel's lead.

But poor Barbara still wasn't smiling when she saw the three boys go into the block of flats – she would have liked to go with them!

A moment later Peter was closing the door of the lift. He was carrying the Father Christmas costume they had picked up out of the gutter. Jack pushed the button, and very soon the three boys were stepping out of the lift on the top floor of the building.

Now where should they go?

Chapter Six

A CALL ON FATHER CHRISTMAS

'Now we go right!' said Colin, taking the lead.

'Yes, but there are *two* doors on the right,' Peter pointed out. 'Which one do we want?'

Jack put his ear to the first door. 'I can hear a radio inside,' he told the others. 'And footsteps.'

Then, all of a sudden, they heard a woman's voice very close to the door. Jack jumped back, startled.

'Oh dear, Grandpa, now where *did* you put your medicine?' said the voice – and it was a trembly, old lady's sort of voice. 'Are you sure you left it on the table?'

'Not very likely he's in there,' Peter whispered. Jack was already listening at the second door.

'I can't hear a thing behind this one,' he said after a moment.

'Well, that's a hopeful sign,' said Colin. 'I shouldn't think he'll want to draw attention to himself after what's just happened.'

'I'll ring the bell,' Peter decided. He made sure he was holding the Father Christmas costume so that it could easily be seen, and then pushed the bell. It rang shrilly. The three boys stared at the door, which might open at any moment.

But nothing moved.

'Are you sure this was the right floor?' asked Jack.

'Yes, absolutely certain,' Colin told him.

Peter pushed the bell again, and once more they heard its shrill ringing sound.

'Just keep on ringing!' Colin advised him. 'He'll jolly well have to open the door if he wants us to shut up. I *know* he's in there!'

Peter grinned, and went on ringing the bell.

At about the twentieth time, they heard a chain being taken off a hook on the other side of the door.

'Yes, he's there all right,' said Colin. 'Carry on!'

At last, almost stealthily, the door was opened a little way, and they saw the young man. 'What is it?' he asked in a quiet voice.

But before Peter had time to open his mouth and tell him, he spotted the Father Christmas costume! His eyes widened in surprise, and then, moving very fast, he flung the door wide open, put out his arm, snatched the costume and slammed the door shut again.

Unfortunately for him, though, Colin had moved even faster – and his foot was in the doorway!

It was a good thing he was wearing a stout pair of shoes, because the young man was desperately trying to close the door again.

'Get out!' he said threateningly. 'Go on, get out of here!'

'We're not leaving without an explanation,' said

Peter firmly.

'We saw it all,' added Jack.

'And we know all about it,' said Colin, untruthfully.

'Know all about what?' asked the young man angrily. 'Go away, will you? You'll be sorry if you don't!'

'You don't frighten us,' Peter replied. 'Our friends are waiting downstairs, and if we're not back in ten minutes they're going to call the police.'

'Police? No – no, not the police!' gasped the wretched man.

'Why not?' said Colin. 'Circulating forged coins – kidnapping – goodness knows what else! I bet you'll have about twenty years in prison.'

'Yes, you won't get out till you're really old,' agreed Peter.

The poor young man had turned quite pale. Of course, the three boys were only bluffing, but their bluff seemed to be working very well.

Just then they heard the sound of the lift coming up to the top floor. 'Quick – come in!' the young man begged them, opening his door again. Obviously he didn't want any trouble with his neighbours.

As soon as Peter, Jack and Colin were inside the small flat, he asked them once again why they had come. 'My mother and father will be back from work in half an hour,' he added. 'They mustn't find you here!'

'That's all right – we'll have left by then,' Peter promised him. 'If you explain why you did it, that is!'

'Explain why I did what? I don't understand any of it myself,' said the young man.

He didn't seem to realize what Peter was talking about.

'What on earth do you mean?' said Colin angrily. 'You go circulating forged coins and you say you don't know anything about it? Stop trying to be clever!'

'Forged coins? What *are* you talking about?' asked the young man. 'I haven't got any forged coins!'

'Then what about these?' said Peter, taking the two he had exchanged for a pound out of his pocket. 'Your friend gave me these this afternoon.'

'But – but there's not a word of truth in it!'

'I told him I wanted change for a pound to give my sister fifty pence to buy our mother a card – didn't you hear me?' said Peter.

'Yes – yes, I do remember now,' the young man admitted. 'But who told you these were forged coins?'

'Listen – they don't sound right, do they?' And Peter jingled the coins close to the young man's ear.

'If you have a metal saw, we can cut one in half,' suggested Jack. 'Then you'll see we're telling the truth!'

'All right, I believe you,' said the unfortunate young man. 'My word – a lot of other peculiar things are beginning to make sense, too!'

He seemed quite stunned as he dropped into a chair, still holding the Father Christmas costume.

'If what you say is true,' he said, 'it certainly explains the way those men went for us just now. It

was such a sudden, unexpected attack!'

'Kidnapping, actually,' said Colin. 'They wanted to get hold of you both. Any idea where those men in the car took your friend?'

'If I knew that I wouldn't be here, would I?' said the young man.

'And what about the money? The fifty-pence coins? Where do *they* come from?' asked Peter, without lowering his voice.

'Why, they're only for giving customers change! My friend takes the cash, gives change if it's needed, and so on – a lot of people will give us two pounds to pay for a photograph costing them one pound ten, so we need plenty of silver for change, that's all. What on earth makes you think I've been forging fifty-pence pieces?'

'And what about your friend?' asked Jack.

'You'll have to ask *him* about that,' said the young man miserably.

Peter didn't know what to say. It looked as if their mystery was as mysterious as ever!

Jack and Colin couldn't think of anything to say, either. All three boys were slightly ashamed of having been so quick to accuse the young man of a crime. They felt sure by now that the two young men, who had seemed so sinister at first in their Father Christmas costumes, were perfectly innocent after all.

'I know!' cried the young man all of a sudden, jumping up from his chair. He was so excited by something that had just occurred to him that he started talking very fast, almost stumbling over his words.

'Didn't you say fifty-pence pieces? Well, what do you think we found in the middle of the woods last week, on the farm road leading to Peartree Farm? Fifty of them! Just left in the grass by the side of the road through the woods there. All we had to do was bend down and pick them up. So those must be your forged coins! We never thought of that. I mean, we didn't see any point in trying to find out who lost them! We went back to work next day outside Bailey's, and we used them for change to give to our customers!'

'We?' asked Colin.

'Michael and me. Michael's my friend, the other Father Christmas, the one you saw kidnapped.'

He stopped for a moment, too upset to say any more. Then he went on. 'I'm Mark. So you see, we didn't really do anything wrong.'

'You should have taken the money you found to the police,' pointed out Peter. 'Then you probably wouldn't be in this mess.'

'I know, but put yourselves in our place!' said Mark. 'It's not every day you find twenty-five pounds lying in the grass. We're pretty hard up, you see – we're students, doing a vacation job to earn a bit of money; Bailey's hired us to stand at their doorway and bring in the customers. We keep the money we make from the photographs, which means we provide our own film too, and that comes expensive for a camera that develops the picture at once. We charge more than the film costs, of course – we have to, if we're to make any profit, but we still have to buy it first, *and* have a stock of change to give the customers. Those fifty-pence pieces went into the bag of change – they were a real windfall.'

'Well, the harm's done now,' said Jack. 'And I'm afraid we're no nearer solving the mystery. We still don't know where those coins come from, or what the connection is between them and the man with the scar, though obviously there *is* a connection.'

'The man with the scar?' said Mark, baffled.

'The man who kidnapped your friend Michael –

and knocked him down outside the shop,' Colin explained.

Mark looked amazed. 'Have you children been on the track of this mystery long?' he asked.

'Only since yesterday,' said Peter, with some pride. 'We don't like wasting time, you see!'

'Look – please don't go to the police,' Mark begged him. 'Something really bad might happen to Michael if you do.'

'Of course we're not going to the police,' said Peter. 'We shall deal with this ourselves!'

'But won't Michael's parents go to the police when their son doesn't come home this evening?' asked Jack, sounding worried.

'They're away on a winter sports holiday,' said Mark. 'Michael was going to join them when our job finishes on Christmas Eve. What are you thinking of actually doing?'

The poor young man sounded rather helpless.

'We'll go to the place where you found those coins,' said Peter. 'They didn't just appear out of nowhere! We may find a trail to follow.'

'But what about tomorrow? What am I going to do tomorrow?' said poor Mark. 'Michael and I have to be at Bailey's every day until Christmas – it says so in our contract! What will they say there, if one of us doesn't turn up and they're short of a Father Christmas?'

'Don't worry, you won't be!' said Colin cheerfully. 'I'll take your friend's place!'

'You?' exclaimed the young man, puzzled.

Peter and Jack were looking startled too.

'Yes, why not? I can't be much shorter than Michael,' said Colin. 'If I find some inner platform soles to put inside my shoes, nobody will notice the difference once I'm in a Father Christmas costume.'

'Good idea!' said Peter. 'And meanwhile the rest of us will go to Peartree Farm.'

'Are you sure there's nothing else we can do?' asked poor Mark.

'Not for a start, anyway,' said Peter. 'I think you'd better get a good night's sleep now – you're going to need to feel fit tomorrow.' And he said goodnight and shook hands with Mark.

'See you tomorrow,' said Colin. 'There's a bus from the village which will get me in here by eight-thirty, so I'll be outside this building at a quarter to nine.'

'Well – thanks very much, all of you!' said Mark. 'See you tomorrow, then!'

He came out on the landing to see the three boys off as they got into the lift.

'And I wonder what tomorrow will bring?' murmured Peter, as they went down to the ground floor again.

Chapter Seven

OUT IN THE SNOW

'You took your time all right!' said George, as Peter, Colin and Jack emerged from the lift a moment later. 'I was just going to come up and look for you.'

'What did he tell you?' asked Pam anxiously.

'Did they make the forged coins themselves?' said Barbara.

'And what about the other young man – where's he been taken?' asked Janet.

Peter replied to all these questions as well as he could, telling George and the girls what the plans for tomorrow were. 'And now it's about time we caught the bus home!' he decided. 'What a good thing we told our parents we were going to stay in town quite late, doing our Christmas shopping!'

The snow was still falling, covering the roads and rooftops. Scamper kept chasing snowflakes on the walk to the bus stop. And when the Seven woke up next morning, the village was covered with a thick white blanket of snow.

Muffled up in warm sweaters, anoraks, woolly hats and scarves, the children met outside Peter and

Janet's house at half-past eight, with their bicycles – all except Colin, that is, who had already set off for the town on the early bus. Usually the children would have been delighted to see such lovely fresh snow – but they had too much on their minds today to think of a snowball fight, or building a snowman.

'And another thing,' said Peter, 'is that all this snow is going to make it difficult for us to find any clues on the way to Peartree Farm.'

White vapour came out of his mouth as he spoke. 'You look like a dragon breathing smoke, Peter!' said Janet, giggling.

But Peter frowned at her, and the others didn't feel like making jokes either. 'Peter's right,' said Pam, sounding dismayed. 'I hadn't thought of that. How can we possibly find *anything* in all this snow? Even if there are any fifty-pence pieces left in the woods beside the farm road, this isn't a good day to go looking for them! They may be quite large as coins go, but we'll never spot them underneath the snow.'

'Well, never mind!' said Jack firmly. 'We're going to go and look anyway – we can't do better than our best!'

Just then Scamper's barking attracted their attention, and they all turned round. The spaniel was outside the door of the garden shed, at the other end of the garden – he must have got out of the house when Peter and Janet left. Janet ran back down the path and tried to make him go in again.

'He's realized we're going on an expedition and he wants to come with us,' said Peter. 'Well, he can't!

59

He'd get soaked and catch cold.'

'Yes – we'll have enough trouble with our bikes,' said Barbara.

'Always supposing the snow-plough's been along that road – it's not one of the main ones,' said George. 'If it hasn't we'll have to walk.'

'Good thing it's been down the village street and the main roads,' said Peter. 'Otherwise Colin couldn't have gone into town on the bus.'

Unable to persuade Scamper to go back indoors,

Janet was still trying to hang on to him. His yelps were pitiful!

'Why don't we take a toboggan?' suggested Jack. 'Scamper could travel on it! Then he'd keep quite dry.'

'What a good idea,' said Pam.

'Well, all right,' agreed Peter. 'But when we can't ride our bikes any more, everyone will have to take turns pulling it.'

No one minded that – they were all very fond of Scamper and hated to leave him behind. So a little later they were on their way, toboggan and all. It turned out that the snow-plough, after sweeping the main roads, had come back to deal with the minor ones, and they found they were cycling along behind it. Each side of the big machine, two great jets of snow sprayed out and fell on the banks. The snow was deeper and deeper the farther out of the village they went, and the children feared they might have to turn back once they left the road cleared by the snow-plough and took the little road to Peartree Farm. Scamper was the only one who wasn't a bit worried – he was travelling in luxury, lying full length on the toboggan with Peter's bike pulling him along!

At just about the same time, Colin arrived at Mark's block of flats. Mark soon came out with the two Father Christmas costumes over his arm, and his camera slung round him.

'No news, I suppose?' he asked at once.

'Well, no!' said Colin. 'It's only just light, you

know! But the others have set off to explore the road to Peartree Farm.'

Then they set off towards the High Street and Bailey's department store. They stopped to put on their costumes in the doorway to the office building in Mill Road, where the two Father Christmasses had changed the day before. A moment later they emerged looking quite different – and who was going to notice that one Father Christmas was rather shorter than the other today?

At last Peter and the others reached the place where the farm road leading to Peartree Farm began. The sky looked heavy, with clouds the colour of lead, and the daylight was a funny, pale colour from all the snow lying on the fields. It was nearly ten o'clock by now. The snow-plough had been crawling along at snail's pace, and of course the children could go no faster.

The snow turned out to be very thick along the farm road. Jack tried cycling along it – and at once his bike sank in half-way up its wheels. Just for a joke, Jack went on pushing the pedals, but soon he lost his balance and fell off into the snow. 'End of the line for bikes! All change!' he cried, laughing, as he got up and knocked the snow off himself.

Peter was the first to get off his bike in the normal way – and he decided they ought to park all the bicycles under a tree.

'At least they'll be in a bit of shelter there,' he said. 'See the look of the sky? I think it's going to snow again.'

And just as he spoke, down came the first few flakes.

'Let's get a move on!' Peter told the others.

So they started down the bridle path. The trees all around them were bowed under the weight of snow. Every now and then some of it slid off and landed on the children's heads as they trudged along. Janet was soon powdered with snow from head to foot. Scamper was very good and sat quietly on the toboggan. It was a long time since he'd seen snow like this!

'We'll never find anything today – it's *worse* than looking for a needle in a haystack!' said Pam. She was trailing along behind the others, feeling cold and getting tired of the whole adventure.

'Cheer up!' said George encouragingly. 'You never know your luck!' But secretly he was rather inclined to agree with her, although Peter seemed determined to press on.

Snow was falling thickly now, and they couldn't see very far ahead of them – so they heard the sound of a motor vehicle long before they could see it.

'Hallo – there's someone else on this path!' said Jack, who happened to be at the head of the procession. 'I can hear a car engine – it's coming towards us.'

'Quick – we'd better hide!' said Peter. 'Whoever's in the car, they mustn't see us!'

The others felt he was right, though none of them, Peter included, could have said why. They ran as fast as they could back into the woods, and crouched down under the trees. The sound was getting louder every moment.

'That's funny – I don't see any wheelmarks in the snow,' whispered Jack. 'And this farm road is a cul-de-sac.'

'A what?' asked Janet.

'I mean it stops at Peartree Farm,' said Jack. 'It doesn't lead anywhere else.'

'Then the car spent the night at the farm,' said George. 'Simple!'

'But the buildings are deserted!' said Jack. 'Mr Fitzwilliam owns some of the land now, and Peter's father farms the rest of it, and the farmhouse is standing empty!'

'Ssh!' whispered Peter, frowning at the other two boys.

The car had just come into sight through the driving snow. It was a big, black car, and inside it the children saw –

'The scarfaced man!' cried Barbara, pressing as close to the trunk of a fir tree as she could.

The car passed by, going very slowly because of the snow. No snow-plough had been up *here*, and no snow-plough would be going to the deserted farmhouse either. The six children were lying flat on the snowy ground. Peter was holding Scamper pressed firmly against him so that the spaniel couldn't make a noise. When he heard the sound of the engine die away, and not before, he cautiously raised his head.

'It's gone!' he said. 'Well – did you see that? The three men we saw in town yesterday!'

'I wonder where they're going?' asked Janet.

'To Bailey's department store!' declared George and Barbara both at once.

'Oh, my word! I do hope Colin will be all right!' said Pam, in a rather frightened voice.

'Don't panic!' said Peter firmly. 'We'll have to trust Colin to look after himself for the moment. What *we* can do is get to the farm and the forgers' hideout – and with any luck we'll find Mark's friend Michael too.'

'Gosh, yes!' said Jack. 'And if you're right, and the deserted farm *is* their hideout, then we'll soon be able to put a stop to their game!'

'They certainly came away from Peartree Farm,' said George. 'So it looks as if that's where they've made their headquarters.'

'And all we have to do is follow their tracks in the snow,' said Barbara. 'Just for once luck's on our side.'

'But what about our own tracks?' said Janet all of a sudden. 'Won't they have noticed *those*?'

'They may have done,' Jack agreed. 'But with all this snow, having to peer forwards with the wind-screen wipers going all the time, I shouldn't think they'll have seen anything at all. After all, they won't have been expecting to see anyone's tracks!'

'Well, let's hope Jack's right,' said Peter. 'But just to be on the safe side, I think we'll keep off the farm road and inside the wood for the rest of the way.'

And he set off, with the others after him. Scamper had jumped back on the toboggan of his own accord, and it was George's turn to pull him along.

They went on like this for about a mile and a half. It turned out to be easier to walk under the trees – the snow didn't lie as thick there as on the road itself.

At last, after about half an hour, they saw the roofs of Peartree Farm ahead as they peered through the snow. Sure enough, the tracks left by the car tyres stopped outside the farm buildings!

'Wait a minute!' said Peter in a low voice. 'Hear that?'

The six children stopped where they were, on the very edge of the wood, and listened.

They could hear a sort of humming noise coming

from the farm – and yet the place ought to be deserted. They had seen the three men leaving! What could this strange sound be?

Chapter Eight

AT PEARTREE FARM

'It sounds like some kind of machine,' said George.

'And it must be coming from inside the farm,' added Barbara.

'I'll scout round and take a look,' Peter decided. 'The rest of you stay here.'

'I'll come with you,' Jack said.

'No, better not,' Peter replied. 'Suppose there's someone there, and they catch me, it's better for just one of us to be out of action!'

Pam shivered, and suddenly thought of Colin. Was he likely to be kidnapped in the same way as Michael? And suppose they lost Peter too? To her own surprise, she felt a tear run down her cheek. How awful – she was crying! She only hoped the others didn't notice!

'You will be careful, won't you?' Janet whispered to her brother. And Scamper growled softly. That was the spaniel's way of offering to go with Peter himself.

'No, you stay here too. Good old Scamper!' said Peter, giving him a friendly pat. Then he left the woods and stepped out into the open. He ran as fast as he could all the way to the farmhouse, flattened himself against the stone wall, and waited for a few moments, listening intently. He couldn't hear anything but the hum of the machinery, somewhere quite close – but there was no other sound, so he hadn't been seen.

After a while Peter crept silently over to the nearest window. 'What luck all this snow muffles the sound of my footsteps!' he thought.

He stopped again, all his senses on the alert, ready to run for it at a moment's notice.

Several seconds went by, and still nothing happened.

Peter moved again – and this time he cautiously leaned forward so that he could see through the window, and looked inside. Then he took up his position in the shelter of the wall again as fast as he could.

But he *had* seen something!

He had seen Michael lying on the floor with his hands and feet tied, and a man sitting beside him. The man's back was turned to the window, so he hadn't seen Peter.

Peter let out a soundless whistle, and leaned over to look in again.

Still hiding in the trees, the other five children watched every movement he made. Their hearts were beating wildly.

'He's spotted something!' said Jack all of a sudden.

'Oh, *what*?' cried poor Pam, on tenterhooks.

'We'll soon find out,' Barbara told her. 'He's coming back.'

Sure enough, Peter was running back to them, taking care to go in the tracks he had already made. The snow was falling as thickly as ever.

'Michael's in there!' he said breathlessly, when he reached the others. 'They've tied him up.'

'The brutes!' said Jack indignantly.

'And there's only one man on guard,' Peter went on. 'We must get him out of the way for long enough to set Michael free.'

'Easier said than done, if you ask me,' grumbled George. 'What did you think of doing – asking him to be kind enough to look the other way while we make off with our friend?'

70

'Well, not exactly!' said Peter, laughing. 'But I think I have an idea. First we must find some pebbles.'

'They'll be terribly hard to pick up with the ground frozen hard like this,' Barbara protested. 'Can't you think of anything else?'

'No, I can't. We haven't got all the time in the world, you know,' Peter told her rather crossly. '*You* think of something else if you like – meanwhile I'm going to get pebbles!'

And he immediately began sweeping the snow away from the foot of a tree. The ground underneath it was rock-hard. Peter could hardly make any impression on it at all when he tried to prise up some small stones.

'Not the best sort of day for digging, I admit,' he said ruefully.

'Scamper!' Janet called suddenly. 'Here, Scamper!'

Scamper came bounding up at once to see what Janet wanted.

'Dig, Scamper!' she told him. 'There's a bone in the ground, a great big bone! Go on, Scamper – seek! Seek!'

Scamper gazed at Janet with his big round eyes, as if he were saying reproachfully, 'Fancy thinking I'd believe a story like that!'

'Seek, Scamper – seek!' Peter urged him.

Scamper stared at *him* as well, but still he didn't budge.

'We want you to kick up pebbles, Scamper,' Peter explained. 'And when we're home, you'll get a bone for them!'

Anyone might have thought Scamper understood every word, and preferred the truth! Because he immediately barked – 'Woof!' – and then began digging away like a bulldozer, front feet working like mad.

'Here's a loose pebble – and another!' cried Jack, picking them up as Scamper's strong claws dug them out of the ground.

When they had a dozen pebbles, Peter told Scamper to stop. 'Thanks, old chap!' he said. 'We've got enough now. And you'll get *two* big bones this evening!'

'With lots of meat left on them!' Janet promised. She gave Scamper a hug, by way of apologizing for telling him a lie just before.

'George, you're going to be the one to throw them,' said Peter, giving his friend the handful of pebbles. 'I want you to attract the guard's attention – get him out here somewhere near the well. Meanwhile Jack and I will nip past behind him and try to make our way indoors and find Michael.'

'Right,' agreed George. 'But the girls can help too. The more of us there are to work on it, the better. If Janet and Barbara and Pam take up positions at different points round the farm, we can throw stones from all directions, and the man won't know where they're coming from.'

'That's not a bad idea,' said Peter. 'All right – share out our ammunition, and then go and station yourselves in good places. As soon as we hear the first stone we'll be ready to move fast!'

And so they did! Less than a minute later, George, Pam, Janet and Barbara were hidden among the bushes round the farm. Peter and Jack were waiting to hear the signal.

Crack! The first stone hit the dilapidated wooden window frame of the room where the guard was sitting.

The children didn't have to wait long before the man appeared in the farmhouse doorway. He looked right and then left, trying to make things out through the snow, which was still falling fast. He couldn't see anything unusual, so he turned to go back inside.

Crack! A second stone struck the wall quite close to the guard. The man whirled round and took several steps down the snow-covered path.

Crack! A third pebble hit the worm-eaten door of the barn.

The guard swerved sideways, startled.

Crack! Crack! Two more pebbles. He must have been wondering if it was snowing stones as well as snowflakes!

'Is he going to go and look or isn't he?' muttered Jack crossly – because unfortunately the man showed no sign of moving away from the house and leaving the way clear for them to go in.

'They're aiming too close to him,' said Peter crossly. 'I *told* them to lure him *away* from the house!'

Crack! The sixth stone hit the top of the old well.

This time the guard saw it fall, and he must have realized that it was only an ordinary pebble, not a gunshot, because he strode forward.

'Come on!' Peter whispered.

And the two boys set off at top speed! Running through such thick snow, they made so little sound that the guard never noticed them – he was too busy investigating the well.

In a moment they were inside the farmhouse, and immediately found the room where Michael was kept prisoner.

'There's no time to explain now!' Peter told him in a low voice. 'We've come to set you free!' And he opened his penknife to cut the cords binding the young man's hands and feet.

'We're friends of your friend Mark,' Jack hurriedly explained, seeing alarm in the young man's eyes.

In a moment the last cord was cut, and Michael was able to rub his sore wrists. 'These people are coiners – they forge money!' he told the two boys. 'I think they're capable of anything! They say that I was circulating some of their coins, and they didn't like it. But it was quite by chance, you see –'

'Yes, you and Mark found them lying in the road last week,' Peter said.

'However do you know that?' asked Michael, puzzled.

'We've been investigating these forged coins for the last three days,' Jack said. 'But what we didn't understand was why the forgers kidnapped you yesterday evening.'

'I told you!' said Michael excitedly. 'I wasn't doing it on purpose, but I was putting their coins into

circulation. They didn't want that sort of advertisement — they haven't finished work on making their forged coins yet, and when they have, they'll circulate them somewhere out of this area.'

'What?' cried Peter, forgetting it would be more sensible to keep his voice down.

'Didn't you hear the noise of the machinery?' And Michael pointed at the floor. Sure enough, the humming sound was coming up from cellars underneath.

'So that's where they coin the money!' said Jack.

'That's right!' Michael managed to get to his feet. 'There are three of them at work there at this very moment. You see that trapdoor? That's how they get down to the cellars where they forge the coins.'

'Well, this looks like a good place for a police trap!' said Peter. 'As soon as we get out of here we'll go straight to the police station.'

'No, don't! You mustn't go to the police, whatever you do!' Michael begged them. 'You see, their accomplices, the other three men, have gone off to town this morning to kidnap Mark too, after he got away last night. And by now my friend's sure to be in their hands.'

'Then so is *our* friend,' said Peter, grimly.

Chapter Nine

CLEVER BARBARA

While Peter was quickly telling Michael the rest of the story, things were happening rather fast outside the farm.

George, Pam, Barbara and Janet had used up all their stocks of ammunition, and Peter and Jack hadn't yet emerged from the farmhouse, with or without Michael. Their friends waiting outside didn't know what to do.

The man was standing near the well, looking suspicious and watchful.

Suddenly Barbara had what she thought was a brilliant idea – dangerous, but brilliant! 'We have to gain time,' she said to herself. 'Whatever happens, we must keep this man out here while Jack and Peter are busy inside.'

And she walked straight out of the bushes to face the man.

Her three friends, still in hiding, stared at her. They had no idea what she was up to.

'Hallo! Getting some nice fresh air?' said Barbara, in a high voice which gave away the fact that she was really trembling with fright from head to toe!

'Just what do you think you're up to, kid?' said the startled guard furiously. 'Throwing stones like that! You might have hit me – what's more, I'll have you know this is private property, and you're trespassing. What you want is a good hiding!' And he raised a huge, threatening hand.

'I'm not scared of *you*!' said Barbara cheekily. 'I bet I can run faster than you can, too!'

By now George had realized that Barbara was trying to keep the man occupied as long as possible. Taking great care, he set off to crawl to the corner of the house through the snow, and then, keeping close to the wall, he managed to go round the back and get into the room where Peter and Jack were talking to Michael.

'Come on!' he whispered breathlessly. 'Barbara's talking to the man out there to keep him busy – but she won't be able to go on for ever. We must do something.'

'There are three more men down there,' Jack told him, pointing to the trapdoor.

'We'll deal with your guard first, I think, Michael,' said Peter. 'And then we'll decide what to do about his friends – with the noise of their machinery, I don't suppose they've even heard us yet.'

Then he told George what was likely to be happening to Colin and Mark. 'Better not mention it to the girls,' he warned. 'There's no need to alarm them just yet.'

George agreed, and then the three boys and Mark

glanced out of the window to see what was happening.

The forger was still standing by the well with his back to them – and astonishingly, Barbara, who was facing the farm, was still carrying on a conversation with him.

'I've got a right to go for a walk if I want to!' she said. 'And this farm *isn't* private property – at least, I know the two people who own it, and they never mind us coming here!'

'It's not good for you to be out of doors in this kind of weather, little girl,' said the forger, trying to sound nice all of a sudden.

And by now Peter, Jack, George and Michael were out of the farmhouse and making their way silently through the snow . . .

Barbara could see them coming up behind the man. She knew she must go on talking.

'Actually I came because I lost something here the other day,' she said.

'Oh dear!' said the man, evidently thinking it best to humour her. 'And what did you lose?'

The fish was biting, thought Barbara. She took a deep breath and went on: 'I lost a ring – you see, I borrowed it from my mother, and then I dropped it down this well.'

'Dear me, that's too bad!' said the man. 'Why didn't you say so before? Well, let's see if we can spot it down there. Was it a valuable ring – a diamond, maybe?' He sounded greedy and hopeful.

He was bending over the opening of the well to see

if he could spot the ring. The four boys were quite close now.

'Can't see a thing!' the man said. 'I'll go and find a torch. Is this well very deep?'

'Not too bad – but deep enough!' said Peter, flinging himself at the man.

The forger swayed, let out a yell, lost his balance, and fell into the well. 'Help! Murder!' he shouted from the bottom. 'Ouch! Help! I'm hurt!'

'Well done!' Barbara told the boys. 'I couldn't have lasted much longer.'

'Well done yourself, Barbara – very *well* done!' said Peter, laughing at his own joke. But Pam and Janet looked rather scared as they emerged from hiding and joined the others.

'Oh, Peter, you might have killed him!' said Pam indignantly.

'No, I mightn't!' said Peter. 'This well's been dried up for ages and I knew it wasn't very deep.'

'There must be enough snow down there to make a nice soft mattress,' Jack added.

'Get me out of here, you kids!' yelled their prisoner. 'Get me out of here!'

'Don't worry,' George told him. 'Just wait a little while, and you'll find the police have good long ladders.'

The man down the well let out a positive roar of rage. 'I tell you, you've broken my arm! It's you the police will be after!'

The children couldn't help smiling. But Peter noticed that every time the man tried to scramble a little way up the side of the well he fell back again, because although there were some handholds, he couldn't grasp them with one hand. If he hadn't actually broken his arm, then he must have sprained a wrist or wrenched his shoulder.

'We've nothing to fear from *him*,' he told his friends. 'Come along, now let's deal with the other three!'

'Other three?' Janet sounded alarmed.

'Down in the farmhouse cellars,' Jack explained. 'That's where they forge their coins. The sound you can hear is the noise of their machinery.'

As they turned back towards the farm, Peter remembered Michael. 'Oh, I haven't introduced you to the others yet,' he told him. 'Michael, this is the Secret Seven Society – minus our friend Colin, that is, but plus our dog Scamper! He's an honorary member.'

Everyone shook hands, and Michael began thanking all the children for coming to his rescue and helping his friend Mark, but Peter cut him short.

'No time for that sort of thing now!' he said briskly, going into the house. 'Come on, we've got to make sure the three forgers in the cellar can't get out, and then go and tell the police.'

The seven of them set to work to pile everything they could find on top of the trapdoor: big stones, wooden beams, some old fire-irons they found in the hearth. Finally they made quite certain that the forgers wouldn't be able to raise the trap from below by adding a blacksmith's anvil which they found in the barn. It was hard work getting it into the house!

'And they never noticed a thing! Good!' said Jack, as they left the farm. 'Now, we want to get into town fast!'

'Yes, there's no time to lose,' said Michael, who was worried about Mark.

'Every second counts,' Peter agreed. *He* was worried about Colin.

Pam was opening her mouth to ask for an explanation. Hadn't they rescued Michael? How could there be any great hurry now? But before she could say anything, they heard the sound of the big black car, quite close to them.

'Everyone into the woods!' shouted Peter in alarm. 'Go on, quick!'

They ran frantically through the falling snow. It bothered Scamper, and he lagged behind. George had to pick him up and drag him to the nearest bushes. No sooner had he joined the others than the big car drew up and stopped outside the farmhouse.

The scarfaced man was the first to get out, and then – 'Oh no!' whispered Pam. She thought she was going to faint!

Janet started trembling all over, and Barbara's teeth were chattering. The boys' hearts fell too, but at least they'd had some warning!

Sure enough, things must have gone exactly as Michael expected. Mark and Colin were in the hands of the forgers. They were still wearing their Father Christmas costumes as they got out of the car, but their beards had been torn off, and the rest of the Seven could see the way they looked round in alarm.

'Oh, I don't believe it!' Pam was saying over and over again, and this time she didn't mind who saw her shed tears. Poor Colin! She couldn't bear to see him a prisoner.

'Now what?' Jack whispered to Peter. 'I'm afraid they've stolen a march on us.'

'Now we must improvise,' said Peter.

'Suppose they find our footprints in the snow?' asked George, worried.

'I don't think that's likely,' said Michael. 'The snow outside the house was all trodden down long before you turned up.'

The children expected that the pile of objects they had left on top of the trapdoor would not go un- noticed – and it didn't. They could hear the scarfaced man shouting angrily as he realized what had hap- pened. A moment later he appeared in the doorway and turned to the two other men, who were on their way in.

'Get those two boys back in the car!' he shouted, pointing to Mark and Colin. 'We've had visitors. Time to get out of here, fast!'

One of the forgers immediately seized Mark and Colin's wrists and forced them into the car again. 'Now, you just keep still, right? And don't do any- thing silly,' he told them. 'Otherwise you'll end up with a bullet through the brain!'

Pam felt terrified when she heard that. She cautiously withdrew a little further into the bushes. The poor girl wasn't feeling at all well.

Meanwhile, inside the farmhouse, the scarfaced man, who seemed to be the leader of the gang, was roaring like a lion. 'Come on, you lot! Can't you use a bit more muscle? Get that thing off the trapdoor –

and fast!'

Obviously they were heaving the heavy anvil out of the way. It made a terrible noise as it crashed sideways on the floor. Then the children and Mark heard the squeal of hinges as the trapdoor was raised, followed by shouts and cries and angry yelling.

A moment later the scarfaced man came storming out of the farmhouse. He stood in the doorway, legs apart, with the snow falling on him. 'Ray! Ray!' he shouted. 'Where are you, Ray?'

And suddenly a plaintive cry came up from the well. The scarfaced man strode over to it. 'The brutes – what *have* they done to you, whoever they are?' he called down.

The children couldn't hear what the man in the well was telling his boss, but they were surprised by the scarfaced man's reaction. He burst out laughing!

'Ha, ha, ha!' he laughed. 'So you let a bunch of kids fool you? You great idiot, Ray – what a stupid thing to do!'

Once his laughter had worn off, however, he leaned over the side of the well again, and this time he sounded angry. 'I've had about enough of you!' he yelled. 'You're hopelessly incompetent – and don't expect *me* to get you out of there! The police can do the job. You'll be behind bars tonight!'

Then he set off fast back to the farm.

There was more shouting, more orders, and then the children found themselves watching, wide-eyed, as the forgers stood in a line and loaded up the boot of the big car with bags and bags of forged fifty-pence coins!

'They're moving out!' said Jack furiously. 'Slipping through our fingers!'

'I'm not so sure of that!' said George suddenly, grinning. 'I've had an idea. Come on! It looks as if loading up the car will take them half an hour or so – and a lot can happen in half an hour!'

Chapter Ten

ADVENTURE ON THE RAILWAY

They needed spades and brooms for George's plan, and they soon found some in one of the farm out-houses. The men who worked for Mr Fitzwilliam and for Peter's father found it convenient to keep some tools at Peartree Farm, for work in the fields and for keeping the farm road in repair. And their equipment came in useful for the children now. They had to shift a great deal of snow, but they worked away with a will – they were racing against the clock!

George's idea was quite simple – they were going to make an artificial snowdrift. That is, they were building up a great depth of snow at a spot where there was a dip in the road. It was hard work, but there were seven of them, and they all did their very best.

They had to go quite a long way into the woods to find fresh snow; they couldn't take it from anywhere close to the farm road for fear of making the scarfaced man and the other forgers suspicious as they drove by. They swept away the marks of their own foot-prints with the brooms.

In about twenty minutes, they worked wonders. When at last they melted away into the woods to watch the forgers go by, no one would have been able to guess at the trap they had set. The whole surface of the farm road was a solid expanse of white. It had been snowing so hard since the black car last came that way that the marks of its tyres were covered up, and snow was still falling to blur any edges left by the children's own snowdrift. It looked exactly like the rest of the road, but the snow lay a metre deep instead of about twenty centimetres!

Hiding behind the trees, they heard the engine of the big car, and soon after that they saw it appear through the curtain of snow, a black and threatening shape.

From their hiding place, they saw that the scar-faced man was sitting in front with the driver and another of the forgers. The three other men, with Mark and Colin, were all squashed into the back.

The car was going slowly, with its back bumper very low and quite close to the snow. Obviously the boot was weighed down with heavy bags of coins.

George felt his heart beating fast. The artificial snowdrift had been his idea, so he felt responsible for what happened next.

The car came on, still as slow as ever. 'Not far now!' thought George in suspense. He crossed his fingers for luck.

The car was going very, very slowly indeed now. 'They haven't noticed a thing!' thought George.

Another five metres . . . another two metres . . .

Splosh!

The big, heavy car went right into the snowdrift and stuck there! All of a sudden, there was snow right up to the bonnet and the windows.

There was a loud crashing noise as the driver changed gear, and then the hissing sound of tyres skidding powerlessly in the deep snow.

The driver changed gear again, but nothing happened. The car stayed just where it was, stuck and unable to move.

This went on for ten minutes, while the driver tried everything – no use! The car wouldn't budge.

Then the forgers got out – they had to push hard to get the doors open, and once out they were up to their waists in snow. They hurried to open the boot and loaded themselves up with as many bags of coins as they could carry. Then they set off through the woods, staggering under the weight of their burden.

Mark and Colin were left in the car.

The rest of the Seven dared not move just yet. They stayed where they were among the trees, in suspense. They longed to rescue the others, but it wasn't safe yet. They never took their eyes off Mark and Colin, who didn't seem to feel it was safe to move either.

Then at last, some while after the forgers had left, when they were quite, quite sure there was nobody else about, they all rushed to the car.

How pleased Mark and Colin were to see them! They could hardly get over it. Colin told the others how the scarfaced man had pounced on himself and Mark in the middle of the crowd, outside Bailey's, and made them get into his car with him. And then it was Michael's turn to tell his friend Mark about his own adventure.

'So now we're all safe and back together again,' said Peter, pleased. 'But this adventure isn't finished yet! We must make sure those forgers are in police custody and out of harm's way.'

'Hear, hear!' said Colin, who was feeling much better now.

'Well, they went off through the snow, and it hasn't snowed enough since then to cover up their tracks,' said Barbara. 'So all we have to do is to follow them.'

And they set off after the fugitives, with Scamper back on the toboggan again. They made their way through the woods, skirted the side of several fields, and then came to a thick pine spinney. The trees grew so close together that it was almost dark underneath them, and the snow had not been able to reach the ground and lie there.

'Bother!' said Michael. 'There are no tracks to follow here!'

'Oh yes, there are!' said Peter, smiling. 'If you happen to have as good a nose as Scamper here, that is!'

He snapped his fingers, and the spaniel jumped straight off the toboggan and rushed up to him.

'Come on, Scamper – good dog! Seek!' said Peter, and the dog set off at once. The Seven, Mark and Michael had to run quite fast to keep up with him.

Sure enough, he led them straight to the place where the trail began again on the other side of the pine wood. 'What a wonderful sense of smell he must have!' said the two young men, patting Scamper. And they went on following the trail.

The forgers had walked through a narrow valley in between the farm fields, and the children followed their path. The snow was falling more thickly than ever now, and there was very poor visibility – so it wasn't until the last moment that the Seven and the two young men saw the huge building looming up ahead of them.

'The viaduct!' said Janet, suddenly realizing that the huge shape was not a building at all. It was one of the piers of the railway viaduct that crossed the valley at this point, before reaching level ground again on the other side.

The Seven and their friends began to run. They *must* catch up with the forgers! And at last they spotted them, just reaching the railway lines that ran over the viaduct. They had taken a path which wound its way up the hillside.

'What are they planning to do?' asked Jack in an undertone.

He was soon to find out. Less than five minutes later they saw a bright light flare up at one end of the viaduct. 'They've lit a fire!' cried Pam, pointing at the flames which blazed up through the snowstorm.

'They must have an explosive of some sort to start a fire so quickly in this snow,' said Michael. 'I think they're going to stop a train, and they've lit that fire on the tracks to make sure the driver sees them.'

'The next train will be the midday express,' said

Colin, who was a train-spotter and knew the local
timetable almost off by heart.

'Suppose they derail it?' cried Barbara, horrified.
'How awful!'

Colin wriggled his wrist out of the sleeve of his
sweater and anorak and looked at his watch. 'It's
nearly five to twelve now,' he said. 'The train stops in
the town at five past twelve, and then it will take
about twenty minutes to get here. That gives us half
an hour!'

They made good use of that half-hour. Peter and Jack cut across the field to reach the road – that took them five minutes – and two minutes later a car came by. The two boys stood in the middle of the road waving their arms, and the car stopped. They got in and told the driver the whole story. The car started off again as fast as it could go in the snow, skidding quite dangerously on the bends.

Within twelve minutes it was in the village and stopping by the Post Office. Peter and Jack ran to the public telephone, and within fifteen minutes they had told their story to their friend the Inspector of Police, who called up reinforcements from the town and the nearby villages. The postmaster, hearing what was up, left his wife to look after the counter and the shop and got out his van to take the boys back to the viaduct – and within twenty-six minutes, Peter and Jack were breathlessly telling the rest of the Seven what had happened.

'The train will reach the viaduct in three minutes forty-five seconds,' Colin told them all, watch in hand.

A little way along the line, the forgers' fire was throwing out sparks. The snow wasn't falling quite as thickly now, and the Seven could clearly see the top of the viaduct. Would the police get here in time to prevent the train from being held up? Would the forgers be arrested?

Colin never took his eyes off his watch. The others gathered around him and listened intently as he did a count-down out loud.

'One minute ten seconds . . . one minute five seconds . . . fifty-two seconds . . . thirty-three . . . thirty . . . twenty-eight . . . twenty-five . . . twelve, eleven . . . seven, six, five, four, three . . . '

Right on time, the midday express appeared at the start of the viaduct. Almost at once, a loud, harsh squeal broke the silence of the snowy countryside – the driver was putting on the brakes and slowing down.

'He's seen the fire – he's stopping!' said Mark, holding his breath.

'Oh, my word!' said Pam. 'I do *hope* nothing dreadful happens!' She could imagine the train coming off the rails and falling over the parapet – she couldn't bear to look. They heard the sound of braking again.

Overhead, right above the viaduct, the clouds parted and let through a pale ray of sunlight to light up the scene, and with a last squeal of its brakes the train came to a halt.

'It's stopped! It's stopped!' cried Colin. Sure enough, the train was now standing quite still on the tracks, just a little way from the fire the forgers had lit. The six men made for it at once – they were holding revolvers. They went up to the driver's cab, and had a discussion with the driver which the Seven weren't close enough to hear. Finally they saw the driver obviously telling the forgers to get into the mail van which was just behind the engine.

Peter and Jack were on tenterhooks. Would the Inspector have had enough time to do anything? Well, they'd soon know now, one way or another!

The scarfaced man opened the door of the mail van. His men were covering him with their guns.

And then, just as he was clambering up into the van, ten or more policemen hidden inside it rushed him. Next moment more policemen leaped out of hiding in the carriage behind it, landed on the lines, and soon had the forgers surrounded.

Down at the foot of the viaduct, the Seven, Mark and Michael shouted with delight. Thanks to them, the police had been able to act. They had reached the railway station in town in time to set a trap!

Now the Seven clambered up the hillside as fast as they could go, to get up to the tracks. They arrived just in time to see the scarfaced man having handcuffs snapped on his wrists. When he saw the

children he looked furious, and glared at them.

The Inspector congratulated Peter and the rest of the Seven. There was still one question to be answered, though. How had the forged fifty-pence coins Mark and Michael found on the farm road got there in the first place? Peter was wondering about this out loud – and one of the forgers, hearing him and knowing he had nothing to lose now, was kind enough to provide the answer!

'That was Ray!' he said. 'He loves sweets, he just can't get enough of them! So one day when the boss wasn't there he put a handful or so of the coins in his haversack and went off to town to stock up. It's an old haversack, though, and the weight of the coins must have made a hole in it. And wasn't the boss furious when Ray told him he must have lost some on his way to town!'

So that explained the little batch of coins lying in the road! It also reminded the Seven of poor Ray, still down the well where his hard-hearted companions had left him, and they told the police that there was another man to be picked up. He would probably be very glad to be arrested, too, and taken in out of the cold. And the Seven decided that when Ray was in prison, they would take him a bag of sweets! After all, it was thanks to him that they'd solved the mystery of those lightweight fifty-pence pieces, and made sure that their new friends Michael and Mark, and the Inspector of Police, and everybody in the adventure except the scarfaced man and his accomplices, had a very happy Christmas.